Go Well,
Anna
Hibiscus!

Books by Atinuke:

Anna Hibiscus

Hooray for Anna Hibiscus!

Good Luck, Anna Hibiscus!

Have Fun, Anna Hibiscus!

Welcome Home, Anna Hibiscus!

Go Well, Anna Hibiscus!

Love from Anna Hibiscus!

You're Amazing, Anna Hibiscus!

For younger readers:

Double Trouble for Anna Hibiscus

Go Well, ANNA HIBISCUS!

by Atinuke

Illustrated by Lauren Tobia

Kane Miller
A DIVISION OF EDC PUBLISHING

Kane Miller, A Division of EDC Publishing

Copyright Page
First American Edition 2017
Kane Miller, A Division of EDC Publishing

First published in 2014 by Walker Books Ltd., London (England)

Text © 2014 Atinuke
Illustrations © 2014 Lauren Tobia

All rights reserved.
For information contact:
Kane Miller, A Division of EDC Publishing
P.O. Box 470663
Tulsa, OK 74147-0663
www.kanemiller.com
www.edcpub.com
usbornebooksandmore.com

Library of Congress Control Number: 2016961409

Printed and bound in the United States of America
1 2 3 4 5 6 7 8 9 10
ISBN: 978-1-61067-679-3

For Grandmummy

A.

To Alice Tobia,

our traveller

L.T.

Anna Hibiscus on the Bus

Anna Hibiscus lives with her mother and her
father, her grandmother and her grandfather,
her aunties and her uncles, her many-many
cousins and her own two brothers, Double
and Trouble. They all live together in a
big white house in a big busy city on the
wonderful continent of Africa.

Millions of people live in Anna Hibiscus's

7

city. Millions of people who shout into their mobile phones, who blow the horns of their cars and taxis and motorbikes, who crash into one another and call, "Yam head!"

Visitors to Anna Hibiscus's city are often so frightened by the noise and wahalla that they turn around and fly straight back to their own countries quick-quick!

Anna Hibiscus is not frightened. Anna Hibiscus was born in the city. She is used to the noise of millions of people shouting. But Grandmother and Grandfather were born in the village. The shouting still gives them big-big headaches!

For Grandmother and Grandfather, home is where there are more goats than people, more trees than houses, more chickens than cars, and no mobile phone signal at-all, at-all.

Now that Grandfather is very old, he has decided that it is time to go back to visit his village. Grandfather says he wants to

be somewhere quiet enough to hear his
memories think.

And today was the day that Grandfather
was going! He was going with Grandmother
and the big girl cousins, Joy and Clarity
and Common Sense. Uncle Tunde was
going to take them there. None of the
aunties and uncles were going. None of the
other cousins were going. Nobody except
Anna Hibiscus.

"Anna Hibiscus!"
Grandmother called.
"Come on! We are
ready to go now-
now!"

"I am coming,
Grandmother!"
Anna Hibiscus
shouted.

Anna Hibiscus's
bag was packed
and she was
almost ready. Now
she was just trying to catch Snow
White. Anna Hibiscus never went
anywhere without Snow
White.

It took a long,
long time to trick
Snow White into
his basket.

"Hurry! Hurry!" shouted Grandmother.
"Hurry! Hurry!" shouted Common Sense.
"Hurry! Hurry!" shouted Clarity.

Grandmother and Grandfather were already sitting in the car! They were sitting in the back with Common Sense and three suitcases.

Uncle Tunde was already in the car. He was in the front with Clarity and five baskets.

Joy was hurrying to the car with Anna's big-big pink bag.

Anna Hibiscus followed her with Snow White's basket.

"Quick, quick!" shouted Uncle Tunde. "Le's go!"

Anna Hibiscus and Joy tried to get into the front of the car with Clarity and Uncle Tunde and the baskets. They tried to get into the back of the car with Grandmother and Grandfather and Common Sense and the suitcases. They tried moving Clarity to the back. They tried moving Grandmother to the front. But whatever they did, Anna Hibiscus and Joy could not fit into the car.

Grandfather groaned. He was hot and his
old bones were uncomfortable.

"Anna and Joy," Grandmother said.
"Maybe you will have to follow
us on the bus."

"Good idea," said
Grandfather. "Le's go!"

So Uncle Tunde
turned on the engine.
The aunties and
uncles and cousins
waved.

13

"Don' cry, Anna Hibiscus," said Joy. "We will follow them on the bus. It will be fun!"

"Don' cry," said Anna's mother. "I went to the village on the bus before you were born. It was fun."

"Don't worry," said Uncle Bizi Sunday. "Follow me!"

It was a long, hot way to the bus station. The many people rushing along the roads pushed and bumped Anna. Snow White's basket and Anna's big pink bag got heavier and heavier. Soon Uncle Bizi Sunday had to carry them. It was not fun.

The bus station was big and dirty.
It was full of thousands of red and
blue and green and yellow buses.
All the bus drivers were sleeping.
All the bus boys were screaming:

"*Kaduna! Kaduna! Kaduna!*"

"*Chad! Chad! Chad!*"

"*Jos! Jos! Jos!*"

It was the bus boys' job to let
everybody know where their bus
was going. And to get as many people
on as possible.

Sometimes even more than possible,
Anna Hibiscus thought!

Anna Hibiscus held tight to Uncle Bizi Sunday's hand. She hoped she would not have to hang out of a window all the way to the village. That would not be fun!

Anna Hibiscus and Joy followed Uncle Bizi Sunday up and down and up and down the rows of buses. At last Uncle Bizi Sunday found a bus that was going the right way. He spoke to the bus boy.

"Make sure they get off at Warra village," Uncle Bizi Sunday said, pointing at Anna and Joy, who were finding seats.

The bus boy shrugged. What did he care? Uncle Bizi Sunday looked worried.

A woman on the bus spoke up. "Who travel Warra way?"

"Mama Eldest's grandchildren travel for dere today," answered Uncle Bizi Sunday.

"Mama Eldest!" A lot of the village women looked at Anna Hibiscus and Joy.

Anna Hibiscus tried to hide.

"Is OK," Joy whispered. "They know
Grandmother, tha's all."

One of the village women leaned over
and pinched Anna Hibiscus's soft cheek.

"Dis one good and fat," she said.

"Thank you, ma," whispered Anna.

Sometimes she wished her cheeks were
not so good and fat!

Then one of the women said, "We go for Warra village. They can follow us."

"Thank you, auntie," said Uncle Bizi Sunday gratefully.

"Thank you, ma," said Joy.

"Thank you!" said Anna Hibiscus.

Anna Hibiscus was glad they had somebody to follow. She did not want to get off the bus in the wrong place. Being lost in the middle of the bush would be no fun at all!

Uncle Bizi Sunday waved good-bye.

"Go well, Joy!" he shouted. "Go well, Anna Hibiscus! Have fun!"

Anna Hibiscus waved good-bye.

She waited for the bus to start. She waited for the fun to start.

It was definitely not fun waiting in a jam-packed bus in the hot-hot sun. Anna Hibiscus started to sweat. Her back sweated. Her face sweated. Her arms and legs stuck to the seat.

Anna Hibiscus wriggled. Why did the bus not hurry up and go? The driver kept on sleeping. The bus boy kept on shouting. And the jam-packed bus kept on getting fuller and fuller and fuller. Now there were two people squashed onto every seat!

A boy with three goats squeezed onto the bus. There was nowhere for him to sit. Anna Hibiscus looked at the goat boy. The goat boy looked at Anna Hibiscus. She still had a whole seat all to herself.

Anna Hibiscus was just about to make room for the goat boy on her seat when a woman with shiny-shiny black hair pushed her way onto the bus and sat down next to her.

Anna Hibiscus did not even have time to move over properly before that woman sat down! Now one of her arms was trapped behind the woman. Anna Hibiscus pulled it out. The woman frowned. Anna Hibiscus frowned too. She eyed the woman and her shiny-shiny black hair.

That hair must be a wig, Anna Hibiscus thought. Women often wore wigs. When they were tired of combing-combing-combing,

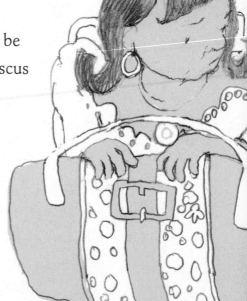

braiding-braiding-braiding and straightening-straightening-straightening their curly-curly hair, then they wore a wig.

Anna Hibiscus frowned again. The woman was squashing Anna Hibiscus on one side. Joy was squashing Anna Hibiscus on the other side. Her legs were squashing Snow White's basket. Anna Hibiscus could

feel Snow White struggling inside.

"Keep still!" the woman hissed.

But it was not Anna Hibiscus who was moving. It was Snow White! He was struggling so much in his basket that he was shaking Anna Hibiscus's legs.

"Can't you sit still!" the woman shouted.

People turned around to look. And just then the lid shot off Snow White's basket and Snow White flew out!

Snow White flew at the first person he saw – the woman shouting at Anna Hibiscus!

The woman saw Snow White flying towards her with his claws and talons outstretched. She stopped shouting and shrieked. The woman jumped up. She fell straight onto the goat boy. He fell onto the floor of the bus with the shiny-haired woman on top of him.

Snow White landed on Anna Hibiscus's head and crowed and crowed. Everybody on the bus laughed. The woman did not laugh. She was shouting at the goat boy now!

One of the goats bent down. It took a mouthful of the woman's shiny-shiny black hair. And the woman's hair came right off in the goat's mouth! Anna Hibiscus had guessed right. That hair was a wig!

Suddenly Snow White snatched the wig from the goat.

The woman stopped shouting. She clutched her real curly gray hair. Then she tried to snatch her shiny black wig back from Snow White. But Snow White was flying too high. Everybody on the bus was laughing and laughing.

23

The woman stood up. She opened her mouth to shout again. Snow White crowed! The woman hurried away to the back of the bus.

Anna Hibiscus looked at Joy. Joy's shoulders were shaking. Joy was trying not to laugh! Anna Hibiscus started to giggle.

Just then the engine of the bus roared into life. The driver had woken up. It was time to go!

Anna Hibiscus giggled and giggled. Joy laughed and laughed. They could not stop! And luckily for them the old bus engine was so loud that the woman could not hear them laughing.

A cool wind blew in through the window of the moving bus. Anna Hibiscus stopped sweating and stretched out her legs. She was no longer hot. She was no longer uncomfortable. She was no longer frowning. In fact, she was still giggling.

Now there was plenty of room for her and Joy on their seats. And plenty of room for the goat boy too. And for his goats.

Riding to the village on the bus was going to be fun after all!

Anna in the Village

Anna Hibiscus was born in Africa. So she knows all about traffic and expressways, all about skyscrapers and shanty towns, all about neon lights and fast food. Because Africa is like that! Anna Hibiscus knows nothing about red dust and thorny bushes. She knows nothing about trees as tall and beautiful as cathedrals. She knows nothing about mile upon mile of banana plantations. And Africa is like that too!

Now the bus carrying Anna Hibiscus and Joy was on its way to the village.

27

"Look!" shouted
Anna Hibiscus.

Alongside the
road were hordes
of cattle with long
pointed horns. The
men herding them
were long and pointed too.

"Meat for the city," the goat boy said.

Suddenly it was dark. The bus had entered
the rain forest. The trees in the rain forest
were so many that their leaves blocked out
all the light. Anna Hibiscus spotted some
antelopes peeping around the trees.

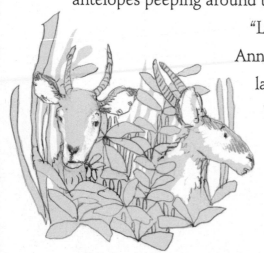

"Look!" shouted
Anna Hibiscus
laughing. "Look!
Look!"

"Bush meat,"
said the goat
boy.

Anna Hibiscus frowned. The bus drove higgledy-piggledy along the bumpy road, a road full of stones and puddles and the wrecks of old cars. Then the rain forest ended. Now there was nothing but banana trees. Then orange trees. Then sugarcane.

Women ran beside the bus with baskets of oranges and sugarcane on their heads.

Anna Hibiscus pointed to the oranges. She was so thirsty! Joy leaned out of the window and bought two oranges and two sticks of sugarcane. Anna Hibiscus chewed her sugarcane all up. She sucked the sweet juice of the orange. Then she remembered the goat boy. Maybe he was thirsty too!

Anna Hibiscus looked at the goat boy.
But he would not look at her. Suddenly the
orange juice in Anna Hibiscus's mouth did
not taste so sweet.

The bus stopped at a town, a small town
with many half-built concrete houses and
a policeman directing the traffic. The bus
stopped next to some women squatting over
cooking fires. The wonderful smell of frying
akara fritters and roasted corn entered the
bus. Many passengers leaned out of their
windows to buy some.

Anna Hibiscus
whispered to Joy.
This time Joy bought
food for three.

"Thank you!" The
goat boy smiled.

He was hungry, Anna Hibiscus thought.
That was why he was always talking
about meat.

Anna Hibiscus pointed at a shop selling
Coca-Cola and white bread. Joy shook
her head.

"What if the bus drives away without us?"
she said.

Anna Hibiscus's eyes widened. She had
not thought of that. That would not be fun
at-all, at-all.

After that Anna Hibiscus fell asleep. Night
came. Joy watched the lights of the towns
they passed, shining in the dark. Then she
too went to sleep.

Suddenly Anna Hibiscus woke up. It was morning. Joy was shaking her. The goat boy had gone. The village women were getting off the bus with their bags and boxes.

"Oya!" they shouted. "Le's go!"

Joy pushed Snow White's basket into Anna Hibiscus's arms. Then she pushed Anna Hibiscus off the bus. The bus drove away in a cloud of dust.

Anna Hibiscus looked around. There were no houses, no farms, no people. There was only dust, red dust flying through the air. And dusty bushes, and stumpy thorn trees growing in red earth. And the only people there were Anna, Joy and the village women.

Anna Hibiscus was confused.

"Where are we?" she asked.

One of the women shrugged. "We are
in the bush!"

"But where is the village?" Anna asked.

The woman pointed. "In the bush,"
she said again.

"Oya! Oya!" said another woman.

The women walked purposefully
into the bush. They walked in
single file, stirring up the dusty
red earth. Joy hurried after them,
carrying Anna's big pink bag.
She pulled Anna Hibiscus
along. The last of the village
women turned around.

"Put your foot where I put my foot!" she said.

"Why?" whined Anna Hibiscus.

It was rude to ask questions when an adult told you what to do. But Anna Hibiscus was still half asleep. She had forgotten.

The village woman sucked her teeth and turned away. She did not answer. But another woman asked over her shoulder, "Do you want to step on a snake?"

Anna Hibiscus woke up properly. She did not want to step on a snake! Definitely not!

Carefully Anna Hibiscus put her foot in the footprint of the last woman in the line. Carefully she put her other foot in the next footprint. Carefully Joy followed in Anna's footprints. Carefully the first woman in the line looked out for snakes.

All morning Anna Hibiscus followed the line of village women trekking through the bush. Her legs ached. The sun burned the back of her neck. The dust settled in her dry throat. But the village women did not tire.

They walked on and on and on.

"Don't they need breakfast?" Anna Hibiscus thought crossly.

Snow White's basket was heavy in Anna Hibiscus's arms. It grew heavier. And heavier. And heavier. Anna's arms got tireder and tireder and tireder. Her feet got slower and slower and slower. The village women were farther and farther and farther ahead. Anna Hibiscus was being left behind!

Anna looked around. Joy was far behind, struggling with the big-big pink bag on her shoulder. Sweat was running down her face.

The village women were walking swiftly a long way ahead. Their loads were balanced gracefully on their heads. Anna Hibiscus was too hot and too tired and too thirsty even to cry. On top of her head Snow White stretched his wings and flapped! He was so light on the top of her head, Anna Hibiscus thought.

And suddenly Anna Hibiscus knew what to do! She shook Snow White off her head. She balanced his heavy basket there instead.

Snow White flew onto it. Then Anna
Hibiscus ran after the village women.

"Anna!" cried Joy. "Stop!"

Anna Hibiscus did not stop. She was
not going to be left behind in a bush full
of snakes!

The village women turned around.
They smiled when they saw Anna Hibiscus
with her basket on her head.

Then they eyed Joy
struggling with her bag
far behind.

"Don' let leopard
catch you there!"
one of them shouted.

Anna Hibiscus
heard Joy shriek.
She watched Joy
put the big-big pink
bag on her head
and run.

The village women
walked on. Anna Hibiscus
giggled and followed
them. Joy caught up.
She frowned at
Anna Hibiscus.

"You know what Mama
and the aunties say!" she hissed.

Anna knew. The aunties said it was
bush to carry things on your head. They said
it as if bush ways were bad ways.

"But we are in the bush now," Anna
Hibiscus said. "We are supposed to do bush
things!"

Anna Hibiscus swung her tired arms.
They were so happy to be free. The basket
was shading her head from the sun! And her
neck felt so strong.

Necks never complained, no matter
what you loaded on top of them. Arms
and shoulders loved to whine. Just like

small cousins when they had to walk.
Anna Hibiscus did not know why anybody
bothered to carry anything with their arms.

Anna Hibiscus walked and walked and
walked. She was tired. She was hungry.
She was thirsty. But she was glad. Because
now it was easy to keep up with the village
women. And Anna Hibiscus did not have to
worry about snakes or leopards or being lost
in the middle of the bush!

Suddenly there was the sound of men
singing!

"Iwe kiko lai si oko ati ada koi pe o koi pe o!"

Anna Hibiscus looked up. Ahead of them were fields! Fields and fields of tomatoes and chili peppers and onions and yams and plantains. And in the fields, men were hoeing the weeds. And while they hoed they sang:

"Iwe kiko lai si oko ati ada koi pe o koi pe o!"

The village women waved and the men waved back. The men put their hoes over their strong shoulders and walked with big steps over the fields. Soon they were walking and laughing with the women.

They looked at Anna Hibiscus and Joy with their dark, serious eyes.

"Mama Eldest's granddaughters," the women explained.

Anna Hibiscus felt shy again with everybody looking at her.

"Look!" said Joy. "The village!"

A small red village was ahead of them. The houses were red. The compound walls were red. The streets were dusty red earth. Anna Hibiscus could hear chickens squawking and goats bleating. She could hear children shouting. They appeared from the houses and compounds. They stared at Anna Hibiscus and Joy.

Anna Hibiscus wished that she could hide. But she had to keep her head up high, otherwise her basket would wobble. And then all the children would laugh at her. Anna Hibiscus walked slowly through the village with her head held high. She had to!

Then she saw Grandmother and Grandfather! They were standing outside a small house. They were waving at Anna Hibiscus!

Anna Hibiscus wanted to push past Joy and the village women. She wanted to run to Grandmother and Grandfather. But Anna Hibiscus knew that if she did that her basket would definitely fall. And then everybody would laugh at her!

Grandfather watched Anna Hibiscus and Joy walking slowly through the village in line with the village women. He smiled.

"They have arrived safely!" he said to Grandmother.

Grandmother smiled too. "They have not only arrived," she said, "they are already walking like true village women."

Anna Hibiscus saw Grandmother and Grandfather smile. She saw how proud those smiles were. Suddenly Anna Hibiscus was proud too.

She had come all the way on the bus. She had trekked all the way through the bush. And now she was walking through the village with her head held high. Anna Hibiscus smiled. She smiled so wide she beamed like the African sun.

Anna Hibiscus Is Brave

Anna Hibiscus is in the village. The village where her grandmother and grandfather were born. She is sleeping in the house her great-grandmother built. It is the home of her ancestors.

Anna Hibiscus woke up. It was morning, but the house was quiet. There were no air conditioners humming, no fans whirring. There were no mobile phones ringing, no traffic was honking. There were no aunties calling, no cousins shouting, no Snow White.

Anna Hibiscus sat up. The other beds in the room were empty.

"Joy?" Anna called. "Grandmother?"

When no one answered, Anna Hibiscus got out of bed. She got dressed. Where was everybody?

Anna Hibiscus peeped into the next room.

"Grandfather?" she whispered.

Grandfather's mat was empty. The room was dark and still. Anna Hibiscus went into the compound.

Grandmother and Joy and Clarity and Common Sense were out in the sunshine. They were shaking baskets of grain in the air.

"Good morning!" Anna Hibiscus called. "Good morning, everybody!"

"Good morning, Anna Hibiscus!" They all smiled.

"Have you seen Snow White?" asked Anna Hibiscus.

Last night, after they had arrived, Snow White had flown off Anna's head. He had chased after some hens. And he had not come back to the compound. Anna Hibiscus had stayed awake a long time in the night, worrying.

Grandmother shook her head. The big girl cousins shook their heads too. Anna's eyes filled with tears.

"Sorry, Anna," Joy said.

"Come and help us with breakfast," Grandmother said kindly.

Grandmother gave Anna Hibiscus a basket of grain and showed her how to shake it so that all the grain flew into the air. The papery shell around each grain blew away. And Grandmother caught the grains in the basket again.

Anna Hibiscus tried. But she was feeling so sad that she did not shake the basket hard enough and the grains did not fly into the air. Just then there was a flap of white wings over the compound wall.

"Snow White!" shouted Anna Hibiscus.
Anna Hibiscus's grains flew high into the
air. They landed on the ground. But it was
not Snow White who landed
on the ground with them.
It was a fat white hen!

Grandmother looked at Anna Hibiscus's
sad face.

"Never mind," she said, putting more
grains into Anna's basket. "After breakfast,
you can go out and look for him."

Anna Hibiscus nodded. She shook her
basket hard. The grains flew into the air.
The papery shells blew away and Anna
Hibiscus caught the grain.

51

"Good," said Grandmother. "Now we must pound the grain."

Anna Hibiscus pounded her grain hard. She pounded it into powder.

"Now we must soak the grain," said Grandmother.

Anna Hibiscus soaked her grain. It turned into a paste.

"Now we can cook the grain," said Grandmother.

Anna Hibiscus helped to gather the firewood. She helped to make the fire. She helped to stir the cooking grain. By now Anna Hibiscus was very, very hungry.

"Now it's ready!" said Grandmother.

Anna Hibiscus took a big spoonful of her breakfast. Oh! Anna Hibiscus coughed and choked. She took a big drink of water.

"Oya, eat! Eat!" said Grandmother.

Anna Hibiscus stirred her breakfast.

Only Common Sense was eating.

"I don't like this breakfast," Anna said at last.

Grandmother smiled. She sprinkled some sugar onto the grain.

"You will get used to it," she said. "There is nothing else."

Anna Hibiscus did not think she could ever get used to it. But she would try.

"Now," said Grandmother, "you big girls can go to the river to wash clothes."

Clarity and Joy and Common Sense clapped their hands happily. All the other big girls in the village would be at the river. And the big boys too.

Grandmother smiled. Then she looked at Anna Hibiscus.

"And you must go out and look for that cockerel," she said.

"Will you come with me?" Anna asked.

"No." Grandmother patted Anna's head. "Because I have work to do here."

Anna Hibiscus crept out of the compound. She crept quietly down the dusty path. She did not want anybody to see her and stare at her again.

Suddenly three village children came running down the path. They had bare feet and torn dirty clothes. Anna Hibiscus was afraid. She wanted to run back to her

compound. But Grandmother would never
let her hide. Anna knew that.

When the children saw Anna Hibiscus
they stopped running.

"Oyinbo!"

one of them shouted.

"Oyinbo! Oyinbo!" the others joined in.

Anna Hibiscus's face grew hot.

"Oyinbo! Oyinbo! Oyinbo!" they all
shouted.

Oyinbo was the word for a light-skinned foreigner. Why were they shouting "oyinbo" at Anna? And why were they shouting it as if it was a bad thing? Anna Hibiscus was confused. Then all of a sudden she felt ashamed. There must be something wrong

with her for the children to shout at her like that.

"Get away from here, you children!" a woman's voice shouted angrily.

The village children ran. Anna Hibiscus ran too. She did not want the woman to see her crying. Anna Hibiscus ran back to her compound.

The gate was open. In the compound Grandmother had her back turned.

Anna Hibiscus ran into the house. She hid underneath her bed.

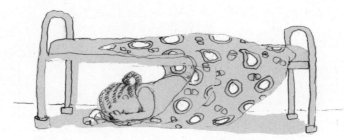

Anna Hibiscus hid for a long time, crying and crying. She wished that her mother would come. But her mother was a long way away, in the city.

"Help!"

Anna Hibiscus heard somebody shout.

"Help me, I beg-o!"

It was Grandmother! Grandmother was shouting for help! Anna Hibiscus crawled out quickly from under the bed.

"*Help!*"

Anna Hibiscus ran out of the house. She ran into the compound. There were many dogs in the compound.

One of the dogs was barking at
Grandmother. The other dogs were eating
the food that
she had been
preparing.

Grandmother
was hiding
behind the
water tank.
Anna Hibiscus
could see she
was shaking.
Anna Hibiscus knew that

Grandmother was
very afraid of dogs.
But Anna Hibiscus
was not afraid. Anna
Hibiscus squatted
down. She opened
a big pan and saw
pieces of meat.

Anna Hibiscus took
out one piece of meat.
She threw it to the
dog that was barking
at Grandmother. The
dog stopped barking.
It ate the meat.

Then Anna Hibiscus walked
out of the compound with the pan. All the
dogs followed her.

Anna Hibiscus threw one last piece of
meat. She threw it far away up the path.
The dogs chased after it. Anna Hibiscus
went back into the compound.
She shut the gate well-well
behind her.

Anna Hibiscus went to the water tank.

"Grandmother," Anna Hibiscus whispered. "You can come out now."

Grandmother peeped out from behind the water tank. She looked around the compound. When she saw the dogs had gone, Grandmother said, "Thank God!"

Grandfather came into the compound smiling happily. He saw Grandmother hiding behind the water tank. He helped her up.

"Wha's goin' on here?" Grandfather asked.

"I was here cooking," Grandmother said. "The dogs came inside. They wanted to attack me!"

"Wha' did you do?" asked Grandfather.

"I hid behind the water tank!" said Grandmother. "What did you want me to do?"

"But the dogs?" asked Grandfather looking around. "Where did they go?"

"I don' know," said Grandmother. "I was behind the tank. I couldn't see anything!"

"I took the dogs out of the compound," Anna Hibiscus said.

Grandmother and Grandfather looked at Anna Hibiscus.

"What?" said Grandmother. "Those dangerous dogs?"

"I was inside the house," said Anna Hibiscus, "and I heard Grandmother shout."

Then she told them what she had done.

"Bravo!" shouted Grandfather. "What a brave girl!"

Anna Hibiscus looked at the ground.

"I am not brave," she said.

Anna was almost crying. Grandmother and Grandfather looked at each other.

"What were you doing inside the house?" asked Grandmother. "I thought you were looking for Snow White."

Anna Hibiscus swallowed.

"I was," she said.  "But the village children called me names. So I went to hide."

"Oh, Anna Hibiscus!" said Grandmother. "Why did you hide?"

Grandfather looked at Grandmother.

"I told you before," said Grandmother. "It is not good to hide."

Grandfather looked at Grandmother.

"Hiding only makes matters worse," said Grandmother.

Grandfather looked at Grandmother. At last he spoke.

"So why were you hiding behind the water tank?" he asked.

Grandmother looked surprised.

"Those were dangerous dogs!" Grandmother said.

Anna Hibiscus looked at Grandmother.

"Grandmother," said Anna Hibiscus quietly. "Those dogs were just hungry. They were not dangerous."

"Anna Hibiscus," said Grandmother crossly, "one was barking and growling at me."

"That is because it knew you were afraid," said Anna softly. "And it knew that because you were afraid, you might try to hurt it."

"How could it know that I was afraid?" asked Grandmother crossly.

Grandfather laughed.

"Ore mi," he said. "You were hiding behind the water tank!"

Then Grandmother laughed too. But Anna Hibiscus still looked sad.

"What name did they call you, my daughter?" asked Grandmother softly.

"They called me oyinbo," Anna Hibiscus whispered.

Grandmother looked at Grandfather.

"Is it true, Anna Hibiscus?" Grandfather asked gently. "Are you oyinbo?"

Anna Hibiscus shook her head. It was not true! Her skin was not white! And she was definitely not a foreigner!

"Then you have nothing to worry about," said Grandfather. "It was only a lie."

But Anna Hibiscus did not feel better. She thought some more. Her skin *was* lighter than other children's skin. Because her mother was white. And part of her *was* foreign. Because her mother and her mother's ancestors were from Canada.

"Maybe it is true," Anna Hibiscus whispered sadly.

"So it is true?" said Grandfather. "Then tell me, Anna Hibiscus. Is it a bad thing to have light skin and to come from elsewhere?"

"Those children said it as if it was bad," Anna said.

"I am asking you, Anna Hibiscus," said Grandfather. "I am asking you what *you* think."

Anna Hibiscus thought again. Then she said, "No. It is not bad. It is not bad to have light skin. It is not bad to come from a foreign country."

Grandfather nodded. "Anna Hibiscus," he said. "We cannot control what other people say to us, or what other people think of us. We cannot control what other people think is good and what they think is bad." He looked gently at Anna Hibiscus. "So we have to be clear about what we think, and what we say."

Grandmother patted Anna's head. "If I can hide behind you next time we meet those dogs," she said, "then you can hide behind me next time we meet those children."

Anna Hibiscus smiled.

"Anna Hibiscus won't need to hide." Grandfather laughed. "She just has to pretend the children are a pack of dogs. Then she will know what to do."

Anna Hibiscus giggled.
And then Snow White
flew into the compound!
He landed on Anna
Hibiscus's head and crowed!

Grandmother and
Grandfather laughed.

"Snow White!" Anna
Hibiscus laughed too.

Anna Hibiscus felt better.

"Who is going to go to the river and call
those big girls home?" Grandmother asked.

"I am!" Anna Hibiscus said happily.

Anna Hibiscus was not sad anymore.
She was not ashamed anymore. And she
was not afraid anymore. With Grandfather's
words in her mind, Grandmother's love in
her heart, and Snow White on top of her
head, Anna Hibiscus felt just fine.

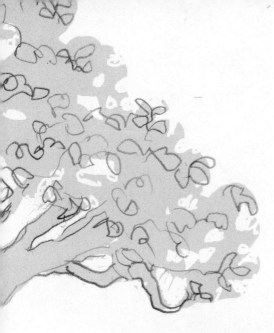

Anna Makes friends

Anna Hibiscus is in the village, the village
of her father's ancestors. She is there with
Grandmother and Grandfather, and
with the big girl cousins, Clarity and
Common Sense and Joy.

Grandfather is happy in the village. He sits
all day under the iroko tree with the other
old men. They talk and laugh about the
things old men like to talk and laugh about.

Grandmother
is happy in
the village.
When she
has finished
cooking in the
compound,
she sits in the cool,
dark house with her friends.

Joy and Clarity and Common
Sense are happy in the village too.
They spend the day at the river, washing
clothes. They
swim and
splash and
laugh with
the big
village boys
and girls.
And Anna
Hibiscus?

Every day Anna Hibiscus helps
Grandmother to sift and pound and cook
grain for breakfast. Anna Hibiscus loves
to eat that grain now. Then Anna helps to
wash the pots, and prepare the beans and
vegetables for dinner. She helps to stack the
firewood and sweep the compound.

But after her work is finished, Anna
Hibiscus has nothing to do.

Anna Hibiscus is not allowed
to sit under the iroko tree with
Grandfather and his friends.
That tree is only for elders.

Anna Hibiscus cannot
follow her cousins to the
river. Big boys and big girls only
want to play with people their own age.

Anna Hibiscus can sit with Grandmother
and her friends. But it is boring listening to
them talk and talk and talk about people
Anna Hibiscus does not know.

So every single afternoon Anna Hibiscus
sits alone in the compound. She watches
Snow White playing with the hens who fly
over the compound wall. She watches
out too for the big red rooster.
He flies over to fight with
Snow White! When he does,
Anna Hibiscus chases him.
She chases the big bad
rooster with a broom,
around and around
the compound until
he flies away.
She does not
want Snow White
to get hurt.

Anna Hibiscus sits and watches and chases every single afternoon. And every single time she looks up, a small boy is staring at her over the compound wall. Anna Hibiscus gives him dirty looks. She does not like being stared at! She does not like big bad roosters! She does not like being left out of all the fun!

"Why won't you let me come wash clothes with you?" Anna Hibiscus begged her cousins one day.

"Why don't you play with somebody your own age?" Clarity asked.

"Are you still afraid of the village children?" asked Joy.

"No!" said Anna Hibiscus. "Not at all!"

It was true. Anna Hibiscus was no longer afraid of the village children. Whenever she saw them she eyed them fiercely. Snow White eyed them fiercely too. And the village children ran away. None of them dared to call Anna Hibiscus names anymore.

"They don't like me!" Anna Hibiscus said.

"What about that boy I always see looking in here?" asked Common Sense.

"I don't like him!" said Anna Hibiscus.

"Oh, Anna Hibiscus!" Clarity laughed.

"He looks nice," said Joy.

"He's always staring at me," growled
Anna Hibiscus.

"So?" asked Clarity.

"It is rude to stare," grumbled Anna.

"Here in the village it is not rude to stare,"
explained Common Sense.

Anna Hibiscus sucked her teeth. All the
big girl cousins laughed. Grandmother shook
her head and went into the house
to sit down.

"Wha's wrong
with Anna
Hibiscus?" asked
Grandfather.

"She is lonely,"
Grandmother
answered.

"Lonely?" said Grandfather.
"This village is full of children!"

"But none of them are her friends," said
Grandmother.

Grandfather went out into the compound.
He found Anna Hibiscus alone.

"Are those children still calling you
names?" he asked.

"No, Grandfather," said Anna Hibiscus.

"So have you been to herd goats with
them?" he asked.

"No, Grandfather," said Anna Hibiscus.

"Why not?" asked Grandfather. "Tha's
what children your age do."

"They have not asked me to go with
them, Grandfather," said Anna Hibiscus.

A dog came to the open compound gate. It looked at Anna.

"You know how to make friends with dogs." Grandfather chuckled.

It was true. Anna Hibiscus had many dog friends. But it was so easy to make friends with a dog. All you had to do was to give it meat and talk kindly to it. But Anna Hibiscus had nothing to give to the village children.

"Grandfather?" Anna Hibiscus asked.

But Grandfather had already gone. Anna Hibiscus could hear him laughing under the iroko tree with his friends.

Anna Hibiscus went into the house.

"Can we go home soon?" Anna Hibiscus asked Grandmother.

"If you want to go home you had better learn those spellings your teacher gave you," Grandmother said.

Spellings! Anna Hibiscus had forgotten those spellings! Her teacher had given her a long and difficult list of words to learn. A list full of words like *cooperation*. It would take Anna Hibiscus days to learn those words.

"You had better start now," Grandmother said.

Anna Hibiscus looked for the list. At last she found it at the bottom of the big-big pink bag. She would have to write the words over and over and over again to learn them. But she had forgotten to pack paper or a pencil!

Anna Hibiscus looked for paper. But she could not find any. Not anywhere. Anna Hibiscus went back outside to sit with Snow White.

"Anna!" Grandmother called her.

"Yes, Grandmother," said
Anna Hibiscus.

Grandmother's friends had arrived.
Anna Hibiscus curtsied to everybody.

"Please bring water," said Grandmother.

"Yes, Grandmother," said Anna Hibiscus
politely.

Anna Hibiscus brought bottles of cool,
boiled water and clean glasses.

"Good girl," said Grandmother. "Now go
back to your homework."

Anna Hibiscus looked at the floor.
Grandmother looked at her.

"Are you learning your spellings, Anna
Hibiscus?" Grandmother asked.

"I cannot find any paper," Anna Hibiscus
said.

Grandmother's friends started to laugh.
Once they started they
could not stop.

They laughed and laughed and laughed.
Tears rolled down their cheeks.

Anna Hibiscus twisted her skirt. Even
Grandmother was laughing! Why?

At last one of the women stood up. "I will
show you paper," she said to Anna Hibiscus.

Anna Hibiscus followed the woman into
the compound. First the woman took a
broom. She swept a small patch of ground
smooth. Then she chose a thin stick from
the pile of firewood.

With the stick she
wrote the letter **X** on
the ground. Then
the woman gave Anna
Hibiscus the stick.
She went back into
the house, still
laughing.

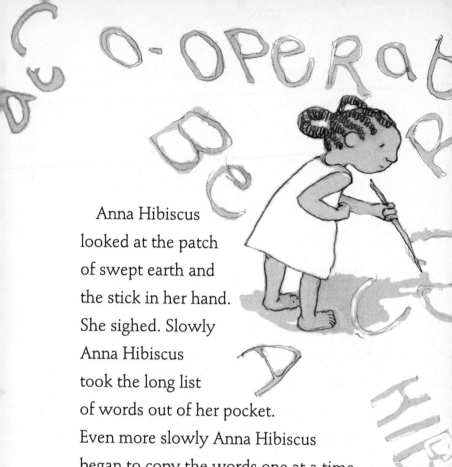

Anna Hibiscus
looked at the patch
of swept earth and
the stick in her hand.
She sighed. Slowly
Anna Hibiscus
took the long list
of words out of her pocket.
Even more slowly Anna Hibiscus
began to copy the words one at a time
onto the ground.

Soon Anna Hibiscus had to sweep more
ground. She copied the words again. Anna
Hibiscus swept and wrote, swept and wrote.
Soon the whole compound was covered
with words.

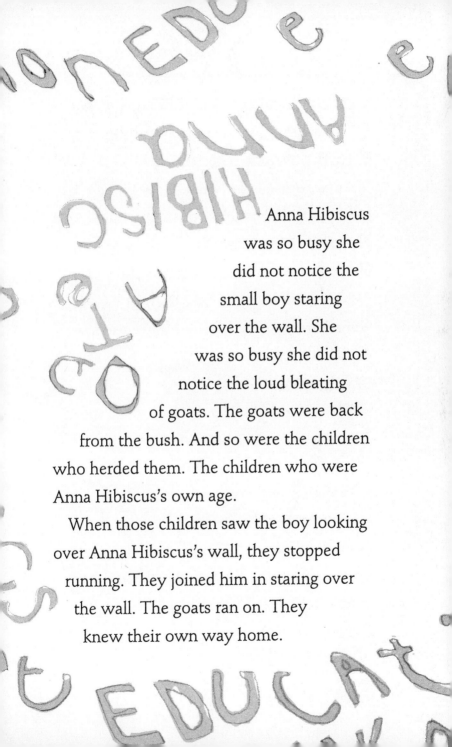

Anna Hibiscus was so busy she did not notice the small boy staring over the wall. She was so busy she did not notice the loud bleating of goats. The goats were back from the bush. And so were the children who herded them. The children who were Anna Hibiscus's own age.

When those children saw the boy looking over Anna Hibiscus's wall, they stopped running. They joined him in staring over the wall. The goats ran on. They knew their own way home.

Anna Hibiscus was bent over the ground.
Opportunity, Anna Hibiscus wrote.
Education, Anna Hibiscus wrote.
Equality, Anna Hibiscus wrote.

Anna Hibiscus frowned. How was she supposed to learn those difficult words? No matter how many times she wrote them, she still could not remember them!

In the middle of writing equality, Anna Hibiscus heard somebody cough. Anna Hibiscus looked up.

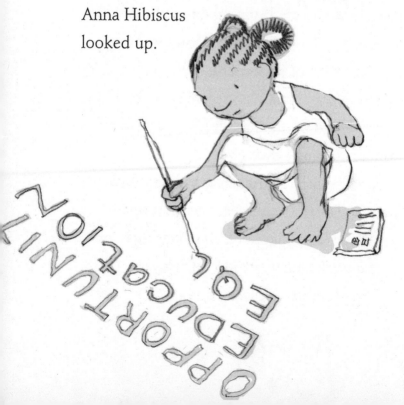

All the village children were staring over
the wall! Anna Hibiscus eyed them fiercely.
But they did not run away. They were not
staring at her. They were staring at the
words on the ground!

Anna Hibiscus bent over. She pretended to
concentrate on writing.

After a while she raised her eyes a little.
Someone was standing in the gateway.
It was the small boy who had been staring.
He was looking at the words.

"Make I learn?" he asked.

Anna Hibiscus hesitated.
Then she gestured to the
firewood. The small
boy chose a stick.
Anna Hibiscus
swept the ground
again. She wrote
a big letter A on
the ground. She
pointed to the letter.

"A," Anna Hibiscus said in a loud voice.
"A." The small boy
copied her in a shy voice.
Anna Hibiscus
nodded. Then she
put her hand over
the boy's hand.
Together they
wrote a big,
shaky letter A
on the ground.

The other children clapped and clapped.
Anna Hibiscus smiled at them. But they did
not smile back. Instead they ran into the
compound. They chose sticks from the pile.
They looked at Anna Hibiscus.

Anna Hibiscus took a deep breath. She
wrote the letter A again. She waited for the
children to copy her. Some of them were
very quick. Others were very
slow. Some of them needed
help. Others could do it
straightaway.

Anna Hibiscus wrote
the letter A over and over
and over until everybody
could get it right.

Anna Hibiscus smiled again.
Nobody smiled back. Anna Hibiscus
blinked back tears. She had given
something to the village children, but they
still did not want to be her friend.

"Until tomorrow?" the small boy asked.

Anna Hibiscus nodded. She would teach the children again tomorrow, even if they did not want to be her friend.

Suddenly the big bad rooster flew over the compound wall. Snow White squawked. Anna Hibiscus shrieked. She grabbed the broom. Around and around the compound Anna Hibiscus chased the big bad rooster. All of the children laughed and laughed.

Then one of the girls
caught Anna Hibiscus's arm.
The girl pulled something
from her pocket. A slingshot!
She fired a tiny-tiny stone at the rooster.
It hit the rooster's tail-feathers. That big bad
rooster flew straight out of the compound.

Anna Hibiscus's eyes grew wide. She had
never seen anybody fire a slingshot before.
The tiny-tiny stone had hit only the rooster's
tail feathers. It had not hurt him, but it had
given him a warning. Anna Hibiscus wanted
to be able to fire a slingshot like that!

The girl showed Anna Hibiscus her
slingshot. She showed Anna how to fit
a stone and aim at the pile of
firewood. Anna Hibiscus
fired. She missed
the wood. She hit a
big black cooking pot
instead! A dent appeared
in the side of the pot.

The children covered
their mouths and
laughed again.

The girl patted Anna
Hibiscus on the arm.
"Don't worry," she said.

"Come out and herd goats tomorrow and we will teach you slingshot well-well!"

Anna Hibiscus's eyes opened wide.

"For true?" she asked.

"Of course," said the girl.

Then the village girl smiled.

The children started to run out of the compound. Their mothers were shouting for them. Anna Hibiscus and the village girls were still smiling.

"See you tomorrow!" Anna Hibiscus shouted.

"Tomorrow!"

The children smiled back, waving their slingshots.

"Anna Hibiscus!" Grandmother rushed out of the house. She was looking at the dent in the cooking pot. Anna Hibiscus did not hear her. She was too busy smiling and waving. Grandmother shook her head, but she was smiling too.

When Grandfather hobbled home from the iroko tree, Anna Hibiscus was waiting for him. She was still smiling.

"Well, Anna Hibiscus?" Grandfather smiled back.

"Tomorrow I am going to herd goats!" said Anna Hibiscus.

"Ahh!" said Grandfather.

"I found something to give to the village children to make them like me," Anna said.

Grandfather raised his eyebrows.

"And did that work?" he asked.

"No…" said Anna Hibiscus slowly. "Actually it did not."

"So what did?" asked Grandmother. "Denting my pot?"

"No," said Anna. "Sorry, Grandmother."

"So?" asked Grandfather.

"They decided to like me when they had to help me too!" Anna Hibiscus said.

"Ahh!" Grandfather smiled again. "That is called cooperation, that is called equality, that is called friendship. Give and take!"

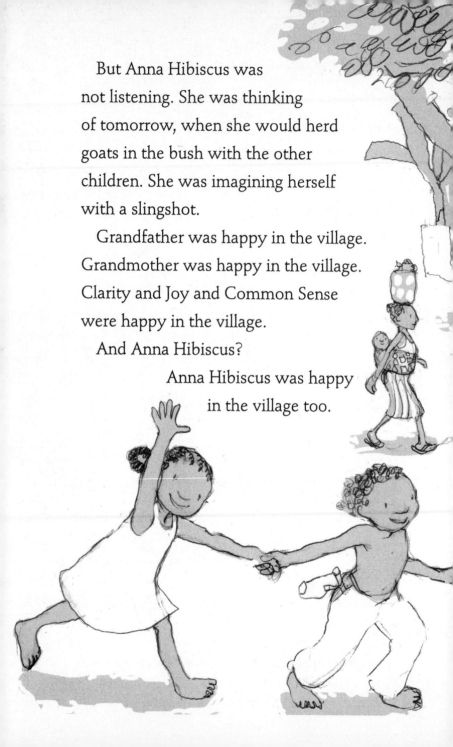

But Anna Hibiscus was
not listening. She was thinking
of tomorrow, when she would herd
goats in the bush with the other
children. She was imagining herself
with a slingshot.

Grandfather was happy in the village.
Grandmother was happy in the village.
Clarity and Joy and Common Sense
were happy in the village.

And Anna Hibiscus?

Anna Hibiscus was happy
in the village too.

Atinuke was born in Nigeria
and spent her childhood in both Africa
and the UK. She works as a traditional
oral storyteller in schools and theaters
all over the world. Atinuke lives on a
mountain overlooking the sea in West
Wales with her two sons.
She supports the charity
SOS Children's Villages.

Lauren Tobia lives in Southville,
Bristol. She shares her tiny house with
her husband and their two yappy
Jack Russell terriers. When Lauren
is not drawing, she can be found
drinking tea on her allotment.